Mickey McGuffin's Ear

written by John Hall

illustrated by Stephen Gilpin

a Red Rocket Bookworks creation

published by

WHITE STONE BOOKS
LAKELAND, FLORIDA

Mickey McGuffin's Ear
Copyright © 2005 John Hall
ISBN: 1-59379-068-6

A Red Rocket Bookworks creation,
Published by White Stone Books
P.O. Box 2835
Lakeland, Florida 33806

Illustrated by Stephen Gilpin
Interior Design by Nancy Bishop

09 08 07 06 05   10 9 8 7 6 5 4 3 2

For every child who has ever forgotten what
their mom said.

For every mom (and dad) who has forgotten what it
was they said in the first place.

For all of my friends at Poplar Grove School who have
waited so patiently (or not) to own a copy of this book.

For Bethany Anne, the most encouraging person I know.

—J.H.

For Nemo, and the way he stares blankly back at
me when I ask him the same question for the third time.

—S.G.

"Momma said something,
last May or November.
Must have been important,
I just can't remember!

I always try to listen
whenever she speaks.
Sometimes I wonder
If my ear has a LEAK!"

"A strange looking thing,
hooked onto my head.
It can hear 'most anything,
(Except sometimes what Momma said...)"

"What is that hole for?
Where does it go?
They say it's real simple,
but do **they** really know?"

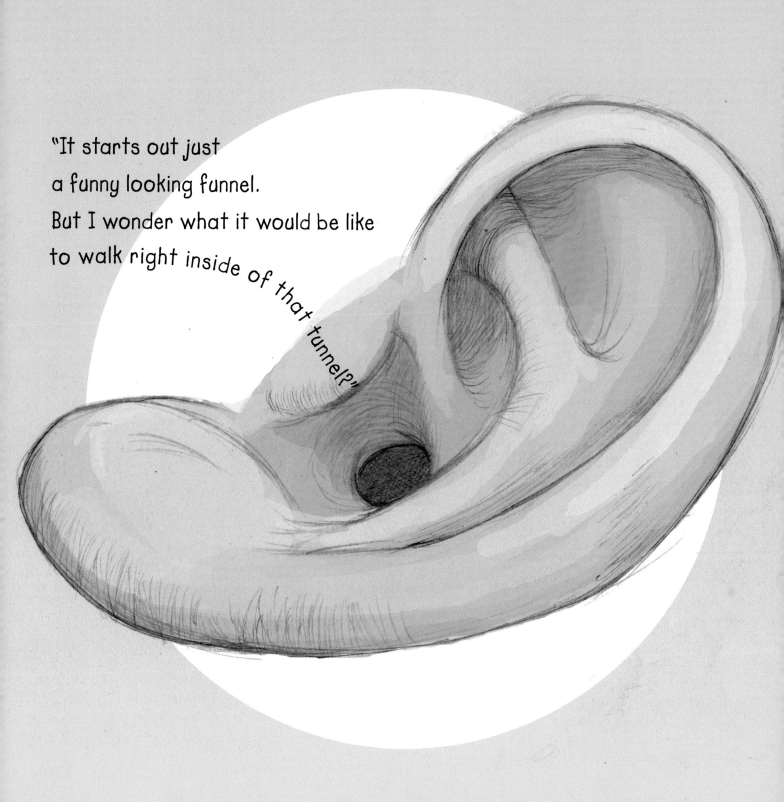

"It starts out just
a funny looking funnel.
But I wonder what it would be like
to walk right inside of that tunnel?"

"If I was real little,
   used some things off my shelf,
   I could climb down inside.
   Take a look for myself!"

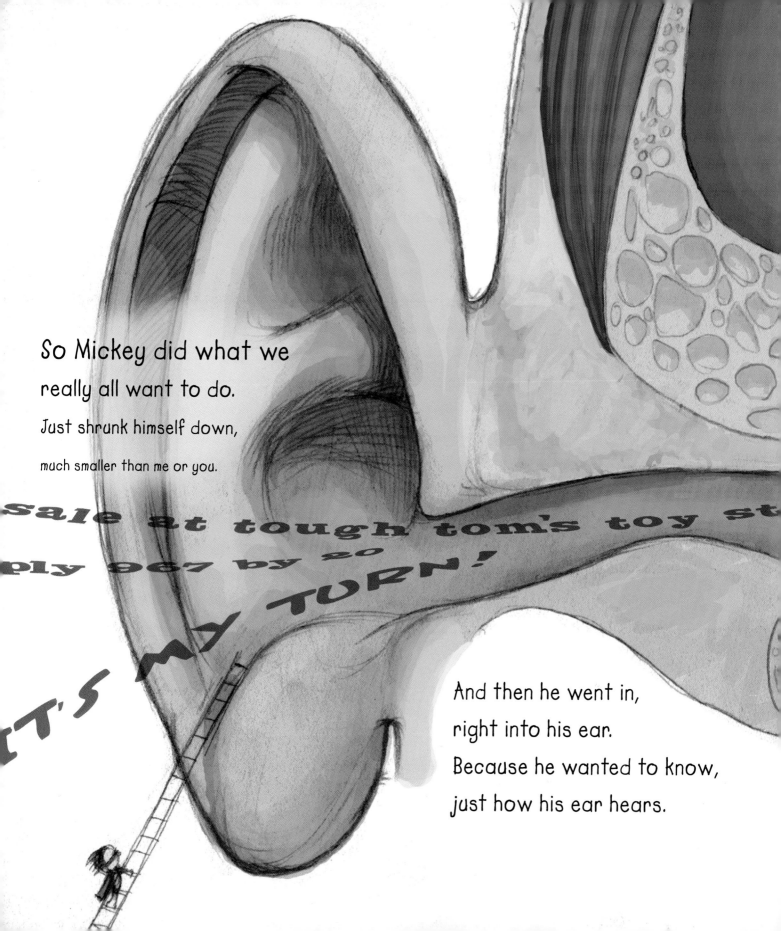

So Mickey did what we
really all want to do.
Just shrunk himself down,
much smaller than me or you.

Sale at tough tom's toy st...
ply 967 by 20

IT'S MY TURN!

And then he went in,
right into his ear.
Because he wanted to know,
just how his ear hears.

"brains"
(extra-large size)

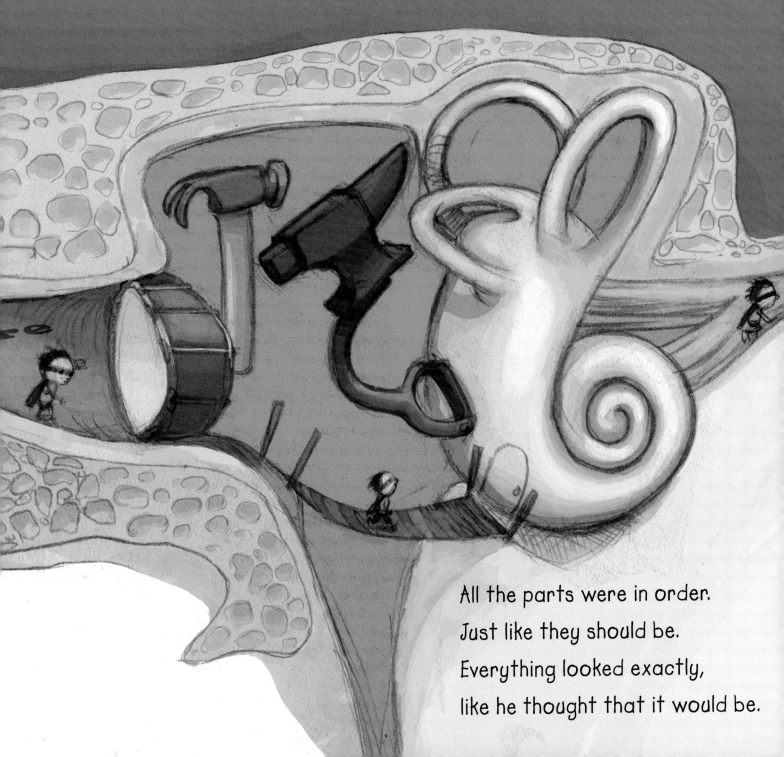

All the parts were in order.
Just like they should be.
Everything looked exactly,
like he thought that it would be.

"Hey, wait just a minute .
What's this ring on the floor?
If I just pull it up,
up comes this secret door!"

So
down
went
our hero,
on
his
sturdy
red
rope.

Right
down
to the
bottom,
at
least
that's
what we hope!

"Now who is that guy?
A friendly enough chap –
but what's he doing in my ear!
I should ask him perhaps."

Then Mickey saw it,
this **was** the right place!
Where things are checked out,
and put in the right space!

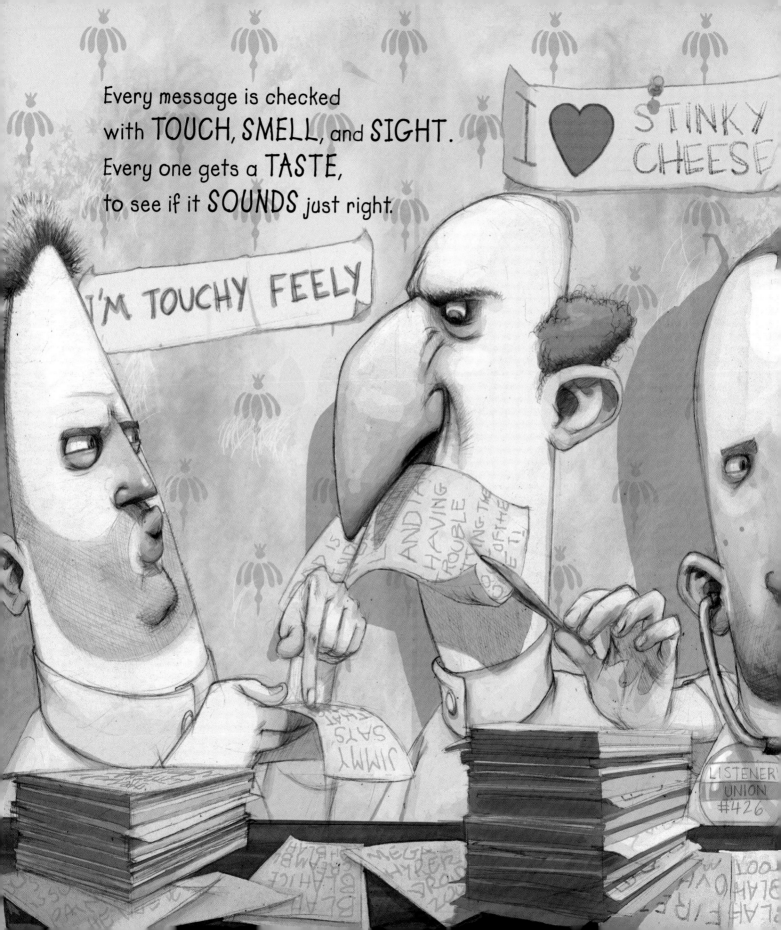

Every message is checked
with TOUCH, SMELL, and SIGHT.
Every one gets a TASTE,
to see if it SOUNDS just right.

Then once they've been checked,
this, that, and every which way,
they absolutely must stop at Harry's
for an absolutely final OK!

"But what happens then, Harry,
after you stamp them OK?
Where do you send them?
I'd like to know if I may."

"I'll tell you now, Sonny.
Follow along, and you'll see.
If you want to find out,
go through door Double B!"

"Behind **Double B**
(just look for the sign),
there's a whole bunch of guys,
most are friends of mine."

"Their job is important,
and they're a little bit crazy.
But one thing they're not—
not one of them's lazy!"

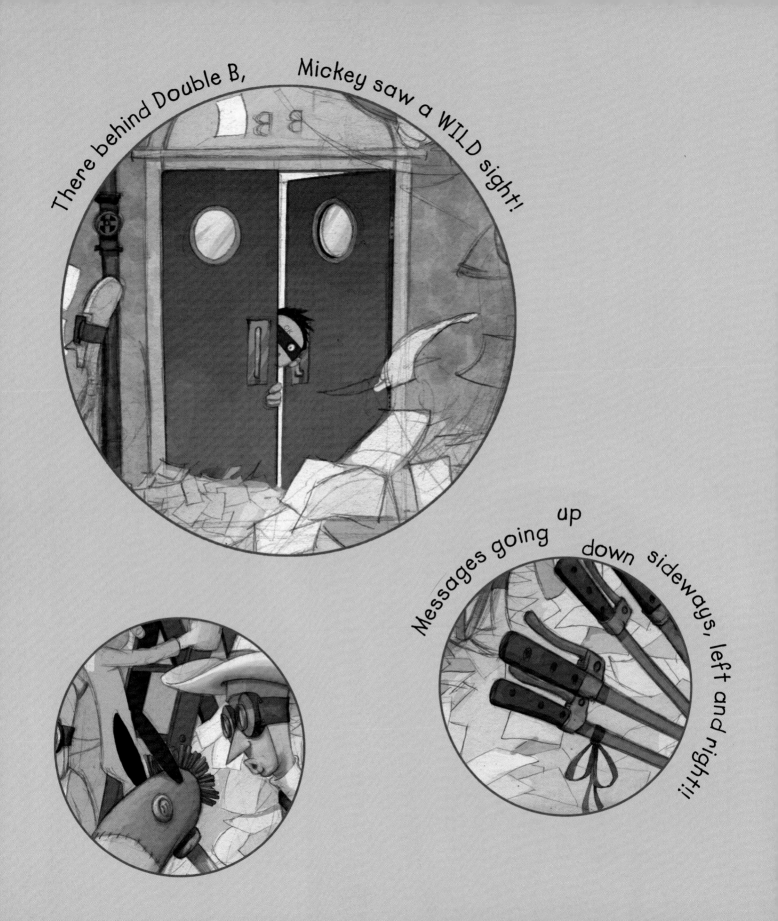

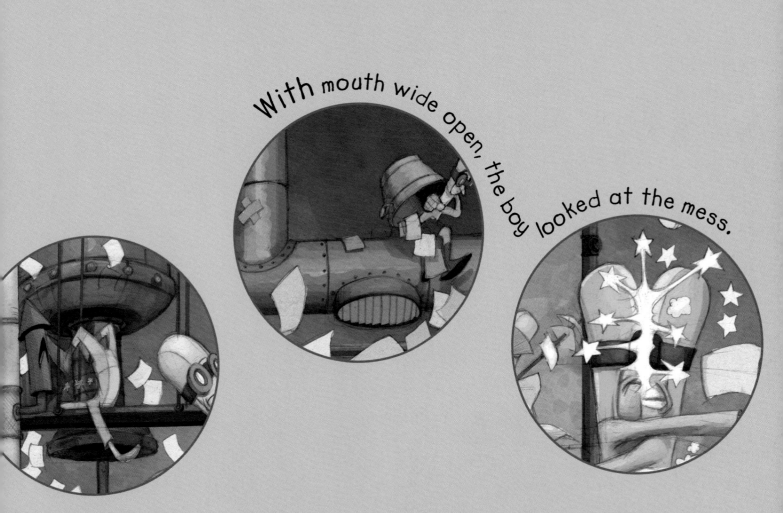

With mouth wide open, the boy looked at the mess.

No **wonder** sometimes it's hard
to listen—**more** or less!

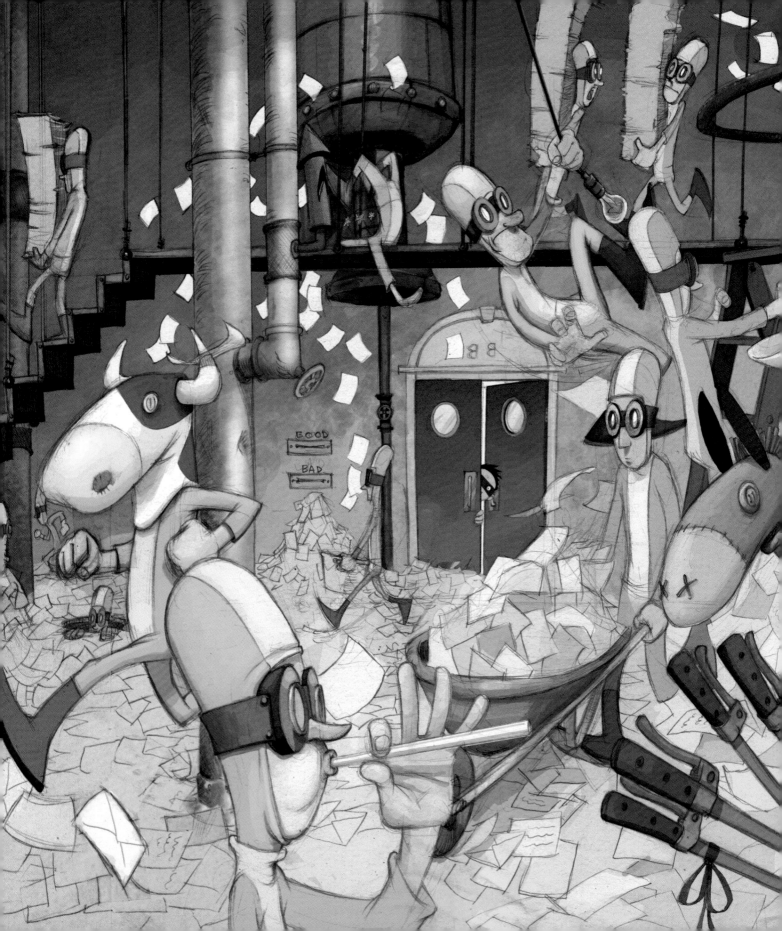

"Hello there, Chappie!
We're the
Double B Bunch.
We'd show you around,
but it's time for
our lunch."

"We work really hard
as plainly you see.
Delivering messages
as fast as can be!"

"We do well together.
We make no mistakes.
We move along fast,
and **never, ever**
take breaks!"

"Hey wait just a minute!
This is MY ear you see.
You'll have to do better
bringing these messages to me!

There must be a way,
much, much better than this.
Some way or the other so
so many won't be
missed!"

"We can't start **changing!**
This is how it's always been run.
But maybe we'll talk about it
tonight when our work
is all done!"

The next thing he knew,
Mickey was sailing through the air.
But it was so much fun,
he really didn't care!

What a ride he was in for
as you will soon see.
Maybe those guys weren't so bad,
those guys Double B.

At last his ride ended.

He shot out with a POP

onto a tall mountain

KERPLOP!

on the top!

"This is really too weird.
Can this really be the case?
That all my messages end up
in the same place!"

"After all that work, everything's piled in a **heap!**?"

Just how do you decide which ones **not** to keep?"

"I have no idea what
these might be about.
I just bag 'em all up
and toss 'em right out."

"If there's anything here
  that's important to you,
I'd grab it right now
    that's just what I'd do."

If you were in his socks,
just which one would YOU pick?

So he skipped news about Legos,
Ignored the funny jokes from Tom..
Instead, he looked around for
what was said by his Mom.

As soon as he grabbed it,
Mickey's brain could recall
every word his Mom said.
It wasn't hard – not at all.

Next thing you know,
he was pulling stuff off his bed.
What do **you** think it was
his **Mom** had first said?

"It's not an easy job
to hear all that stuff.
For someone my age,
listening has got to be rough!"

"Maybe I should talk to those guys.
Be tough, leave no doubt.
Tell them they have to shape up
Or SHIP OUT!"

"But now that I'm thinking
oh my, oh dear!
Never wondered about this..."

"How exactly do **they** hear !?"

Coming Soon from

Red Rocket  Bookworks

Coming January 15, 2006

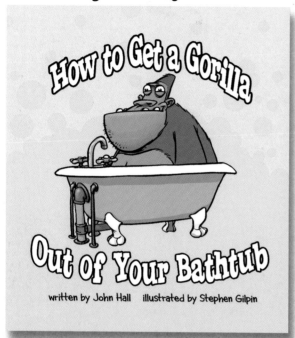

How to Get a Gorilla Out of the Bathtub
1-59379-070-8

Coming March 15, 2006

If the Earth had a Zipper
1-59379-069-4

WS

WHITE STONE BOOKS
LAKELAND, FLORIDA